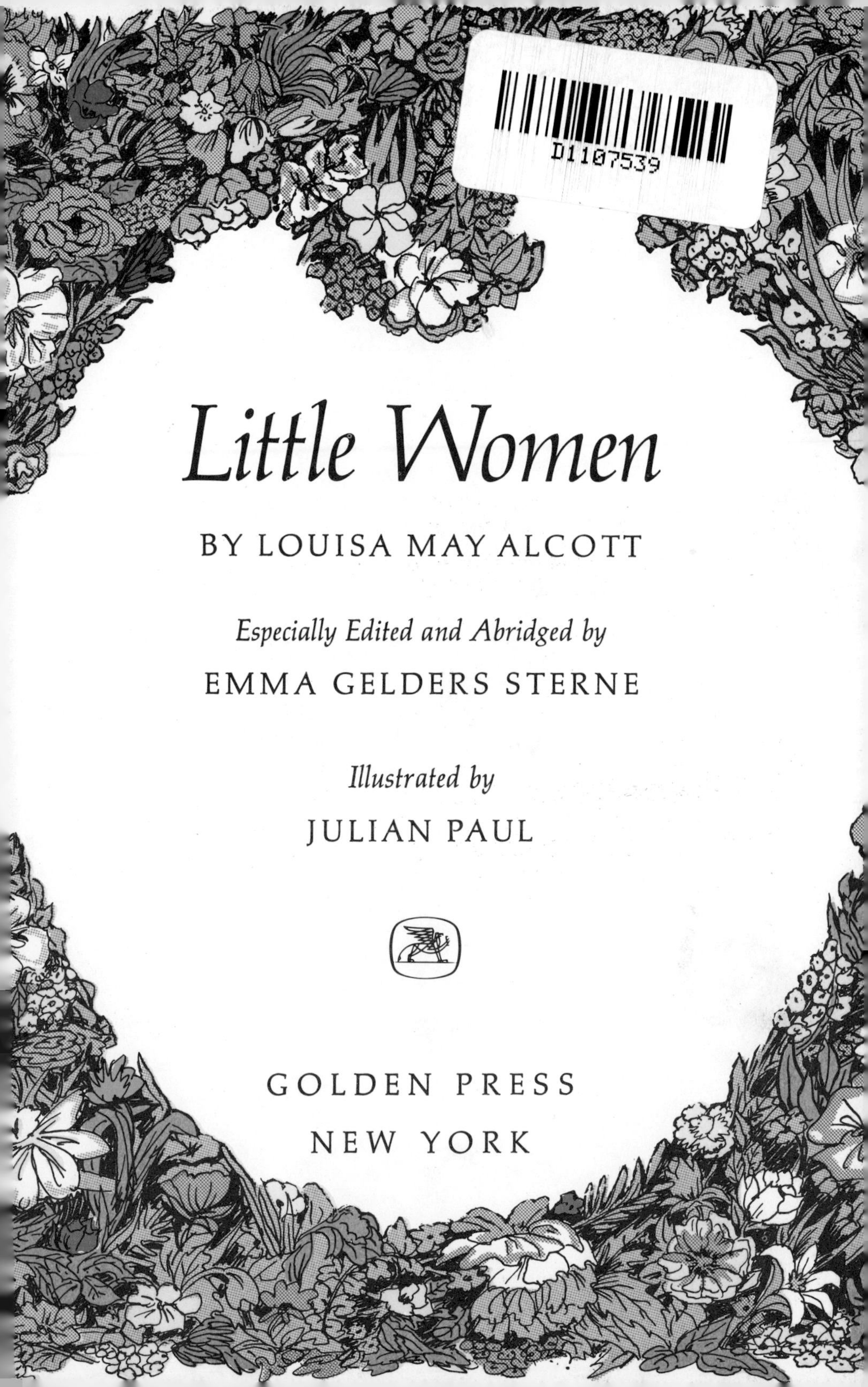

Little Women

BY LOUISA MAY ALCOTT

Especially Edited and Abridged by

EMMA GELDERS STERNE

Illustrated by

JULIAN PAUL

GOLDEN PRESS
NEW YORK

Contents

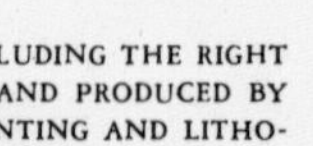

 DESIGNED AND PRODUCED BY ARTISTS AND WRITERS PRESS. PRINTED IN THE U.S.A. BY WESTERN PRINTING AND LITHOGRAPHING COMPANY. PUBLISHED BY GOLDEN PRESS, INC., ROCKEFELLER CENTER, NEW YORK 20. PUBLISHED SIMULTANEOUSLY BY THE MUSSON BOOK COMPANY, LTD., TORONTO.

Playing Pilgrims

"CHRISTMAS won't be Christmas without any presents," grumbled Jo, lying on the rug in front of the blazing hearth. The firelight shone on her dark hair and cast shadows on her thin, brown face. She kicked up her heels in a most unladylike fashion. But fifteen-year-old Josephine March cared nothing about being ladylike. She had always regretted not being born a boy and now, when the Civil War was raging in the land, she felt this regret more than ever.

"You know the reason Mother proposed not having any presents this Christmas," sighed Meg, the oldest of the four March girls. "She thinks we ought not to spend money for pleasure when our men are suffering so in the Army. We can't do much, but we ought to make what little sacrifices we can."

"It's so dreadful to be poor," little Amy pouted. "I don't think it's fair for some girls to have plenty of pretty things and others nothing at all."

"We've got Father and Mother and each other," said Beth.

"We haven't got Father," said Jo, thinking of their father, far away where the fighting was. "And I don't think the little we'd spend on Christmas will do any good to the soldiers. I agree not to expect anything from Mother or from you girls, but we've each got a dollar, and I do want to buy that book of adventure tales I've wanted so long."

"I had planned to spend mine for new music," sighed Beth.

"And I need drawing pencils most awfully!" Amy exclaimed.

Let's each buy what we want and have a little fun. I'm sure we work hard enough to earn it," cried Jo.

Meg nodded. "I know I do—teaching those tiresome King children all day."

"You don't have half as hard a time being a governess as I do shut up with fussy old Aunt March for hours," Jo answered.

" I do think helping Hannah with the housework and washing dishes is the worst work in the world," sighed Beth. "My hands get so stiff I can scarcely practice on the piano."

"I don't believe any of you suffer as I do." Twelve-year-old Amy shook her yellow curls in despair. "You don't have to go to school with girls who laugh at your patched dresses."

As Meg jerked out her knitting needles and began work on a blue woolen army sock, the clock struck six. Beth jumped up and put her mother's house slippers by the hearth to warm.

"Those slippers are quite worn out," Meg said. "Marmee must have some new ones."

"I thought I'd get her some with my dollar," said Beth.

"No, I shall!" cried Amy.

"Let's each get her something for Christmas," suggested Beth.

"Capital!" exclaimed Jo. "What shall we get?"

"Gloves," said Meg, looking at her own pretty hands.

"The slippers from me," said Jo.

"Some handkerchiefs, all hemmed," said Beth, who at thirteen was an accomplished needlewoman.

"I'll get a bottle of cologne," said Amy. "With Marmee's presents and our play, it will be a merry Christmas after all!"

"Glad to find you so merry, my girls," said a cheery voice at the door, and Mrs. March came into the room.

As they gathered about the table for supper, Mrs. March said, "I've got a treat for you."

A quick, bright smile went round like a streak of sunshine. Beth clapped her hands, and Jo tossed her napkin in the air, crying, "A letter! A letter from Father!"

"Yes, a nice, long letter. He sends loving wishes for Christmas and a special message to you girls."

I know my girls will be loving children and will do their duty faithfully so that when I come back home I may be prouder than ever of my little women.

Mrs. March folded the letter soberly. "Do you remember how you played Pilgrim's Progress when you were younger? You'd travel with bundles on your backs from the cellar, which was the pilgrim's City of Destruction, up, up—"

"To the top floor where our burdens fell off and tumbled downstairs. Then we'd go on with light hearts—"

"Till we came out on the flat roof that was Christian's Celestial City. We'd look down on the treetops and flowers and sing for joy!"

"And have cake and milk," Amy added. "If twelve years old wasn't too grown-up, I'd like to play it over again."

"We are never too old to play Pilgrim's Progress," her mother answered. "We play it all the time in one way or another. Our burdens are here, our road is before us. Suppose my pilgrims begin—not in play but in earnest—till Father comes home. Each of you has her burden—Meg, her work; Jo, her temper; Amy, her selfishness . . ."

"Beth hasn't any," Jo interrupted.

"Yes, I have," sighed Beth. "Mine is dishes and envying girls with nice pianos and being afraid of people. Before you came home, Marmee, we were in the Slough of Despond."

"And you pulled us out, as Help did in Bunyan's book," said Jo, delighted with her mother's plan. "We ought to have our roll of directions, like Christian. What shall we do about that?"

"Look under your pillows on Christmas morning," answered Mrs. March.

A Merry Christmas

Jo was the first to wake in the gray dawn of Christmas morning. She slipped her hand under her pillow and drew out a little crimson-covered book. It was that beautiful old story of the best life ever lived, and Jo felt it was a true guidebook for any pilgrim.

Meg's book was bound in green, Beth's was dove-colored, and Amy's, blue. Their mother had written a few words inside each book, which made the presents very precious, and the girls resolved to read a few passages every day.

When the east grew rosy with the coming day, Jo and Meg put aside the books and ran downstairs. Hannah was there before them, building up the kitchen fire. The presents for Mrs. March had been hidden under the sofa in a basket.

A bang of the street door sent the girls to the table, eager for the festive breakfast.

"Merry Christmas, Marmee! Thank you for our books. We mean to read from them every day," they cried out in a chorus. "Breakfast is ready!"

"Merry Christmas, my dears. But I want to say one word before we sit down. Not far away from here lies a poor woman with a little newborn baby. Five children are huddled into one bed to keep from freezing, for they have no fire. The oldest boy came to tell me. My girls, will you give them your breakfast as a Christmas present?"

There was a moment's silence broken by Beth. "May we go and help carry the things?" The others began piling the steaming, fragrant buckwheat cakes and bread into a basket. Hannah was already gathering firewood in her arms.

They were soon ready, and the procession set out through back streets to the bare, miserable room that was the Hummel family's home.

"Ach, it is good angels come to us," murmured Mrs. Hummel.

"Angels in boots and mittens and cold noses," answered Jo.

That was a very happy breakfast, and when they went home to their own bread and milk, there were not in all the town four merrier people than the hungry March girls who had given away their Christmas breakfast.

"Three cheers for Marmee!" cried Jo, as Meg escorted their mother to the table.

Mrs. March smiled with her eyes full of tears as she examined her presents. The slippers went on at once; a new handkerchief, well scented with Amy's cologne, was slipped into her pocket; and the new gloves were pronounced a perfect fit.

By the time breakfast was over, the morning was almost gone and the rest of the day was devoted to preparation for the play. Scenery was made from cardboard, gorgeous robes from old cotton and silver paper. Armor was covered with bits of tin garnered from the pickle factory. The stage was set in the big spare bedroom, and the folding bed let down to serve as seating space for the audience.

At dusk, a dozen girls from the neighborhood piled on the bed and sat before the chintz curtain in a most flattering state of expectancy. Behind the curtain there was a good deal of whispering and a giggle or two from Amy. At last a bell sounded, the curtains flew apart, and *The Witch's Curse: An Operatic Tragedy* began.

Thrilling scenes followed, one by one. A witch's cave was replaced by a towering castle which unfortunately tottered and fell with a crash that cut short the love scene of Act II. The third act was played in the castle hall where the villain drank from the poison cup prepared for the hero, and, after a good deal of clutching and stamping, fell flat and died. A fourth and a fifth act followed in which all ended happily for the two lovers, Roderigo and the fair Zara.

Tumultuous applause ended only when the folding bed began slowly to close on the audience. The actors came to the

rescue, and all were taken out, laughing and unhurt. The excitement had hardly subsided when Hannah appeared, with "Mrs. March's compliments and would the ladies walk down to supper."

This was a surprise even to the actors, and when they saw the table, they looked at one another in silent amazement. There was real ice cream—two great bowls of it, pink and white—and cake and fruit and handsome French bonbons. And in the middle of the table, four great bouquets of hothouse flowers!

"Is it fairies?" gasped Amy.

"It's Santa Claus," said Beth.

"Aunt March?" guessed Jo.

"All wrong. Old Mr. Laurence sent the supper," replied their mother.

"The Laurence boy's grandfather? What in the world—we don't even know him!" exclaimed Meg.

"You mean the people who live in the big house next door?" asked one of the guests. "My mother says he's very proud and doesn't like to mix with the neighbors. He keeps his grandson shut up when he isn't walking or riding with his tutor, and makes him study dreadfully hard."

Mrs. March explained. "Hannah told his gardener about your breakfast party. Mr. Laurence sent me a nice note this afternoon, saying he hoped I would allow him to express his friendly feeling toward my children by sending a few trifles in honor of the day."

"That boy put it into his head. I know he did!" cried Jo. "He's a capital fellow, and I wish we could get acquainted. I spoke to him once when Beth's cat jumped over the garden hedge. I mean to know him someday for he needs fun. I'm sure he does," declared Jo, as the plates went round, and the ice cream began to melt out of sight.

Pleasures and Burdens

"Jo! Jo! Where are you?" cried Meg, at the foot of the garret stairs.

"Up here!" answered Jo's voice from above. Meg found her on an old sofa eating russet apples and crying over a sad story. This was Jo's favorite refuge. Here she loved to retire to enjoy the quiet and the society of a pet rat who lived near-by, to read, or to write page after page of her own "book."

As Meg appeared, Scrabble, the rat, whisked off, and Jo looked up to hear the news.

"We've an invitation from Mrs. Gardiner for a party tomorrow night. Marmee is willing we should go. Now, what shall we wear?"

"You know we'll wear our poplins because we haven't anything else. Yours is as good as new, but there's that awful scorched spot in the back of mine where I burnt it," said Jo.

"You must sit still all you can and keep your back out of sight," Meg declared firmly.

On New Year's Eve, Mrs. March and the two younger girls stood at the door watching Meg and Jo depart for the dance, with Hannah to escort them to the door. They looked very nice in spite of a few mishaps—Meg in silvery gray with a blue velvet snood, lace frills, and a pearl pin; Jo in maroon with a stiff linen collar, and a white chrysanthemum as her only ornament. No matter that Meg's high-heeled slippers were very tight and hurt her.

"Is my sash right?" asked Meg, as she turned from the looking glass in Mrs. Gardiner's dressing room. "Now then, Jo, don't forget to keep the back of your dress out of sight, and *do* act ladylike."

Down they went, feeling a little timid, for they seldom went to parties. Meg was asked to dance at once and went tripping away on her high heels so briskly that no one would have guessed the pain their wearer suffered. Jo felt a little forlorn left alone, but when she saw a red-headed youth coming toward her, she fled into a curtained recess, intending to watch in peace. Unfortunately, another bashful person had chosen the same refuge, for as the curtain fell behind her, she found herself face to face with the Laurence boy!

"I didn't know anyone was here!" stammered Jo, preparing

to back out as hastily as she had come in.

The tall, black-eyed boy laughed. "Don't mind me; stay if you like. I only came in here because I don't know many people and felt rather strange."

"So did I," said Jo. "Don't go away, please, unless you'd rather."

They stood for a moment in awkward silence. Then Jo said primly, "I think I've had the pleasure of seeing you before. You live near us, don't you?"

"Next door." The boy laughed outright, for Jo's prim manner was rather funny and so unlike her everyday self. "How is your cat, Miss March?"

"Nicely, thank you, Mr. Laurence. But I'm not Miss March. I'm only Jo."

"And I'm not Mr. Laurence. I'm only Laurie. My name is Theodore, but I don't like it, so people call me Laurie."

"Mine's Josephine, and I hate it. I wish everyone would call me Jo."

"Do you like to dance, Miss Jo?" he asked.

"I like it well enough, but not tonight. I told Meg—that's my sister, Margaret—I wouldn't, because—"

"Because what?" Laurie asked, as Jo stopped short.

"Well, I have a bad trick of standing before the fire, and I burned my frock. Meg told me to keep still so the scorched spot wouldn't show. You may laugh if you want to. It's funny, I know."

But Laurie didn't laugh. "Never mind," he said. "There's a long hall beyond here. We can dance grandly there, and no one will see us."

The hall was empty; Laurie danced well and taught Jo a new step, so that she thoroughly enjoyed herself. When the music stopped, they sat on the stairs and talked until just before supper when Meg appeared in search of her sister.

"I've turned my ankle in these stupid slippers. It aches terribly. I don't know how I'm ever going to get home."

"Those silly heels! It's too bad," said Jo. "I don't see what we can do."

Laurie immediately offered his grandfather's carriage to take them home.

So after a gay supper together, they rolled away in the closed carriage feeling very festive and elegant. Laurie rode on the box with the coachman so Meg could keep her foot up. By the time Jo had finished telling her adventures, they were home, and eager voices were crying out, "Tell about the party!"

Meg's foot was quite recovered the morning after the party, but she woke up out of sorts. It did seem hard to have to take up work again after the gay holiday. She was fond of luxury, and her chief trouble was poverty. When she turned sixteen, she had begged to be allowed to work and had found a place as nursery governess. But at her work, she saw every day the kind of life she fancied. She tried not to be envious, but she could not help contrasting her shabby dresses and workaday world with the fine clothes and parties of the lively, older girls in the King household.

Jo had happened to suit their wealthy old great-aunt, who

was lame and needed a companion. This sort of work did not suit Jo at all, but to everyone's surprise, she got on remarkably well with her tempestuous relative. The real compensation for the hard work at Aunt March's was a large library of fine books, in which Jo spent many happy hours while the old lady was napping.

Aunt March and the Kings were burdens to be borne, surely, and the girls did not look forward to beginning again after the holidays.

Hannah stalked in and laid two hot turnovers on the table. These turnovers were an institution in the household. The girls called them "muffs," for they had no others, and found the hot pies very comforting to their hands on cold mornings. Hannah never forgot them, no matter how busy or grumpy she might be.

"Now then, Meg!" Jo tramped out the door, feeling that the pilgrims were not carrying their burdens as well as they might. Meg followed in silence, but before turning the corner, they looked back. As always, there was their mother at the window, nodding and smiling and waving her hand to them.

The Laurence Boy

"WHAT IN THE WORLD are you going to do now, Jo?" asked Meg one snowy afternoon, as her sister tramped through the hall in rubber boots, old coat and hood.

"Going out for exercise," answered Jo, with a mischievous twinkle in her eyes. She was flourishing a broom in one hand and a shovel in the other.

With great energy Jo began to dig a path in the new-fallen snow all around the garden. Beyond the low green garden hedge, rising high on its hilly slope, was the stately stone mansion of the old gentleman, Mr. Laurence.

To Jo, this fine house seemed a kind of enchanted place, full of splendors no one enjoyed. She had long wanted to behold the hidden glories and to know the Laurence boy. Since the Gardiners' party she was more eager than ever; but a week had gone by, and she had not caught a glimpse of him. As she dug her snowy way to the hedge, she made her plans. Mr. Laurence was out—she had seen him drive off. The servants were out of sight—no human was visible except the black-haired boy looking wistfully out of an upper-story window.

Jo picked up a handful of soft snow and aimed it straight for the big house. The eyes at the window brightened, the lips widened in a smile.

"Are you sick?" Jo called out.

Laurie opened the window and croaked hoarsely, "Better, thank you. Bad cold. Been shut up all week."

"I'm sorry. What do you amuse yourself with? Do you read?"

"Not much. They won't let me."

"Can't somebody read to you?"

"Grandpa does sometimes—and Brooke. He's my tutor. Can't ask them all the time, though."

"Have some friends come and see you, then."

"Don't know anybody."

"You know us," began Jo.

"So I do! Will you come, please?" cried Laurie.

"I'll come if my mother will let me. I'll go ask her." And Jo shouldered her broom and marched into the house.

A few moments later she was ringing the Laurence doorbell and asking for "Mr. Laurie." A surprised servant came running up to Laurie's parlor to announce a young lady.

"All right. Show her up. It's Miss Jo," said Laurie.

"Here I am, bag and baggage," she said briskly. "Mother sent her love. Meg wanted me to bring some of her custard, and Beth thought her cats would be comforting. I knew you'd laugh, but I couldn't refuse—she was so anxious to help."

Beth's furry loan was just the thing, for in laughing over the kittens, Laurie forgot his bashfulness.

"Shall I read aloud?" Jo asked, eyeing a row of inviting books.

"If you don't mind, I'd rather talk."

"Not a bit," Jo answered gaily. "Beth says I never know when to stop talking."

"Is Beth the rosy one who stays home?"

"Yes, that's Beth."

"The pretty one is Meg, and the curly-haired one is Amy."

"How did you find that out?"

Laurie colored up. "I often hear you calling to one another, and when I'm alone I can't help looking over at your house. When the lamps are lighted, before the curtains are drawn, it's like looking at a picture—to see the fire and all of you around the table with your mother. I can't help watching, though I beg your pardon for being so rude. I haven't any mother."

The look in his eyes went straight to Jo's warm heart. "We'll never draw that curtain any more," she said. "I just wish you'd come over and see us. Would your grandfather let you?"

"I think he would. He's just afraid I might be a bother to strangers—"

"But we aren't strangers. We're neighbors." Jo talked on and gave him a lively description of their household and of their great-aunt for whom she worked and the library where she snatched precious hours for reading.

"If you like books so much, come down and see ours. Grandpa is out, so you needn't be afraid," said Laurie.

"I'm not afraid of anything," returned Jo, tossing her head.

"I don't believe you are!" the boy exclaimed admiringly and led the way down the stairs and through the house. When they came to the library, Jo clapped her hands with delight. The room was lined with books, and there were pictures and statues and a great open fireplace. Suddenly a bell rang, and Jo exclaimed with alarm, "Mercy me! It's your grandfather!"

"What if it is? You're not afraid of anything, you know," returned Laurie, looking wicked.

It was not Mr. Laurence, however, but the doctor who had

come to see Laurie. The boy excused himself, "Would you mind if I left you for a bit?"

"Not at all. I'm happy as a cricket here." She was standing before a fine portrait of old Mr. Laurence when the door opened again. Without turning, she said, "I'm sure now I wouldn't be afraid of him. He's got kind eyes though he looks as if he has a tremendous will of his own! He isn't as handsome as my grandfather. But I like him."

"Thank you, ma'am," said a gruff voice behind her and there, to her dismay, stood Mr. Laurence. Poor Jo blushed till she couldn't blush any redder.

"So you're not afraid of me, hey?"

"Not much, sir."

"And you don't think me as handsome as your grandfather?"

"Not quite, sir."

"And I have a tremendous will, have I? But you like me in spite of it?"

"Yes, I do, sir."

Her answers pleased the old gentleman. "You've got your grandfather's spirit, if you haven't his face," he said. "He was a brave man and an honest one, and I was proud to be his friend."

Then he asked in a sharper tone, "What have you been doing to this boy of mine?"

"Only trying to be neighborly, sir! He seems a little lonely. We're only girls, but we would be glad to help if we could, for we haven't forgotten the splendid Christmas present you sent us," answered Jo eagerly.

"Tut, tut! That was the boy's affair. I shall come and see your mother sometime. Tell her so. There's the tea bell. Come down and go on being neighborly."

"If you'd like to have me, sir."

"Wouldn't ask you, if I didn't," Mr. Laurence barked, and offered his arm. Laurie came running downstairs. He started in surprise at the sight of Jo on the arm of his grandfather, marching in triumph down to tea.

When they rose from the table, Jo proposed to go, but Laurie led her to the conservatory and cut an armful of roses and heliotrope. "Please give these to your mother and tell her I like the medicine she sent me very much."

They found Mr. Laurence in the drawing room standing before the fire. But Jo had eyes only for the grand piano. "Do you play?" she asked Laurie.

"Sometimes."

"Play for me now, so I can tell Beth."

So Laurie played—and remarkably well.

Beth Finds the Palace Beautiful

When all the afternoon's adventures had been told, the March family felt inclined to go visiting in a body, for each found something very attractive in the big house on the other side of the hedge. Mrs. March wanted to talk of her father with the man who had not forgotten him. Meg longed to walk in the conservatory among the flowers. Beth sighed for the grand piano, and Amy was eager to see the fine pictures and statues.

"It's like Pilgrim's Progress," said Beth. "We got out of the Slough of Despond and up the steep hill by trying to be good, and the house over there may be our Palace Beautiful!"

But Beth could not get up courage to enter the Palace Beau-

tiful. Somehow word of her timidity came to Mr. Laurence's ear and he set about mending matters. During one of the brief calls he made, he led the conversation to music and told such gay stories that Beth came out of her corner to listen.

She came closer and closer until she stood, wide-eyed, in back of his chair. The artful old gentleman took no more notice of her than if she'd been a fly. Presently, as if the idea had just occured to him, he remarked to Mrs. March, "Laurie is neglecting his music now, and the piano suffers for want of use. Wouldn't some of your girls like to run over and practice on it now and then, just to keep it in tune, ma'am?"

Beth took a step forward and pressed her hands together. She had heard that the Laurences' grand piano had beautiful tone. The thought of practicing on that splendid piano quite took her breath away.

"They needn't see or speak to anyone," the old gentleman went on. "Please tell the young ladies what I said, Mrs. March. They are most welcome to use the piano. If they don't care to come, never mind."

With a nod and a smile, he rose to go, and Beth made up her mind to speak.

"Oh, sir, they do care, very, very much," she said softly.

"Are you the musical girl?" he asked, as if he were just aware of her presence.

"I'm Beth. I love it dearly, and I'll come if you're quite sure nobody will hear me play."

"Not a soul, my dear."

"How kind you are." Beth slipped her little hand in his. She could not think of any words to thank him.

The old gentleman softly stroked her hair and said in a tone few people ever heard, "I had a little girl once with eyes like these. God bless you, my dear. Good day, ma'am." And away he went in a great hurry.

Next day, after two or three retreats, Beth went in by the side door and at last touched the great instrument. What beautiful sound came from it! She forgot her fears and after that first happy hour, the little brown hood slipped through the hedge nearly every day. She never knew that old Mr. Laurence often opened his study door

to hear the sweet tunes, or that Laurie stood guard in the hall so that she wouldn't be disturbed, or that the new, easy pieces found themselves on the piano just for her.

"Marmee," Beth said one evening, "I'm going to work Mr. Laurence a pair of slippers. I don't know any other way of thanking him. Can I do it?"

The pattern was chosen—a cluster of pansies on a purple background—and Beth embroidered early and late until the slippers were finished. With Laurie's help they were smuggled onto the old man's study table with a short, simple note.

All day passed and the next before any acknowledgment came from the big house. On the afternoon of the second day, Beth went out on an errand. As she came up the street on her return, she saw three heads popping in and out of the parlor windows.

"Here's a letter from Mr. Laurence! Come quick!" several voices cried.

At the door her sisters seized Beth and bore her to the parlor. The shy girl turned pale with delight, for there stood a little cabinet piano with a letter addressed to "Miss Elizabeth March" lying on its lid:

Miss March:
Dear Madam—

I have had many pairs of slippers in my life, but I never had any that suited so well as yours. Pansies are my favorite flower, and these will always remind me of the gentle giver. I like to pay my debts, so I know you will allow me to send you something which once belonged to the little granddaughter I lost.

Your grateful friend and humble servant,
James Laurence.

Amy's Catastrophe

ONE Saturday afternoon Amy found Jo and Meg getting ready to go out with an air of secrecy that excited her curiosity. When she found out that Laurie had invited the older girls to go to the theater to see *The Seven Castles,* she insisted upon going along.

"It's impossible, Amy, because you aren't invited. Next week you can go with Beth and Hannah—" Meg explained. But Jo snapped impatiently, "You can't go, so don't be a baby and whine."

Jo's tone and manner angered Amy. As the two girls hurried down, she called over the banisters, "You'll be sorry for this, Jo March. See if you aren't."

"Fiddlesticks!" returned Jo, slamming the door.

On the way home, Jo wondered idly what Amy might have done to get even. Last time the younger girl had soothed her feelings by turning Jo's top bureau drawer upside down on the floor. But today, when they opened the front door, all seemed quiet, and Amy sat in the parlor reading. Jo decided that her little sister had forgiven and forgotten the quarrel.

There Jo was mistaken. Next day, when she went up to the garret to write a chapter in her book, the manuscript was not in its accustomed place. She raced downstairs and burst into the parlor. "Has anyone taken my book?" she demanded breathlessly.

Meg and Beth said "No" at once. Amy poked the fire and said nothing.

"Amy, you have it!" Jo said fiercely.

"No, I don't."

"You know where it is, then!" cried Jo, taking her by the shoulders and giving her a slight shake.

"You'll never see your silly book again," declared Amy. "I burnt it up."

"What! You burnt my book! My book I worked over and meant to finish before Father got home?"

"I burnt it yesterday! I told you I'd make you pay for being so cross."

Amy got no further, for Jo's hot temper mastered her, and she shook the child till her teeth chattered, crying, "Amy March, you are a wicked girl! I worked very hard for weeks on my book! I never can write it again. I'll never forgive you as long as I live!" she shouted.

With a parting box on her sister's ear, Jo rushed out of the room up to the old sofa in the garret to sob out her grief and anger alone. Jo's book was her pride. It was only half a dozen tales but she had put her whole heart in the work, hoping to make something good enough to print.

When the tea bell rang and Jo appeared, Amy said meekly, "Please forgive me, Jo. I'm very, very sorry."

"I shall *never* forgive you," was Jo's stern answer.

All evening and all the next day she looked like a thundercloud and ignored Amy entirely.

"Everybody is so hateful, I'll ask Laurie to go skating," said Jo, and off she went.

Amy watched them leave with an exclamation of disappointment. "Jo promised I could go with her the next time she went skating."

"It's hard for Jo to forgive the loss of her precious book," said Meg, "but I think she might be friends again if you try her at the right minute. Go after them and wait until Jo is feeling cheerful, skating with Laurie. Then ask her forgiveness again."

"I will," said Amy, and after a flurry to get ready, she ran after Jo and Laurie who were just disappearing over the hill. Both had their skates on before Amy reached them, and Laurie was sounding the ice. When Jo saw Amy coming, she turned her back.

"I'll go on to the first bend to see if it's safe before we race," Laurie called.

Jo heard Amy fumbling with her skates, but she made no sign and zigzagged slowly down the river. Her anger had grown until it had taken possession of her.

As Laurie turned the bend, he shouted back, "Keep near the shore; it isn't safe in the middle."

Jo glanced over her shoulder. "No matter whether Amy has heard or not," her little demon of anger said, "let her take care of herself."

Jo was just at the bend when she saw Amy, far behind, skating out toward the smooth ice in the middle of the river! Thoroughly frightened, she turned back just in time to see Amy throw up her hands and go down with a sudden crash of melting ice and a cry that made her sister's heart stand still. Laurie rushed past and called out, "Get a rail! Quick!"

How they did it, she never knew, but somehow they got Amy out of the freezing water, more frightened than hurt. Shivering, dripping, they walked the child home and finally put her to sleep, rolled in blankets.

During the bustle Jo had scarcely spoken. She had flown about looking pale and wild, her dress torn, her hands bruised. When Amy was comfortably asleep and the house was quiet, Mrs. March, who was sitting by the bed, called Jo to her to bind up the hurt hands.

"Are you sure she is safe?" whispered the unhappy girl.

"Quite safe."

"Laurie saved her," Jo sobbed. "If she had died, it would have been my fault. I let her go! It's my dreadful temper. I try to cure it, but then it breaks out worse than ever. Oh, Marmee, what shall I do? What shall I do? I really feel terrible about it."

Amy stirred and sighed in her sleep, and Jo looked up with a troubled expression on her face. "I let the sun go down on my anger. I wouldn't forgive her, and today if it hadn't been for Laurie, it might have been too late!"

Secrets

THE summer was a busy and happy one. Work mingled with play made the long days seem short.

The girls had not forgotten their play at being pilgrims. One afternoon Laurie was swinging idly in a hammock when he saw the Marches come out of their house as if bound on an expedition. They carried long staffs, and each one had a linen bag slung over one shoulder. They walked quietly out the little back gate and began to climb the hill that lay between the house and the river.

"Well, that's strange!" said Laurie to himself. "To have a picnic and not ask me!"

Having nothing better to do, he roused himself to follow

and see what the girls were up to. A grove of pines covered one part of the hill, and here he caught sight of the four sisters, busily knitting and sewing.

Laurie advanced slowly. "May I come in, or shall I be a bother?"

"Come in, of course," Jo said at once, "but we'll put you to work. You can finish this story I'm reading aloud while I set the heel of my sock."

"It's against the rules to be idle here," Meg explained. "We bring our work here to be out of doors. For the fun of it, we bring our things in bags on our backs and carry staffs like pilgrims."

"I know," Laurie said. "Beth told me about your game of Pilgrim's Progress."

"We call this hill the 'Delectable Mountain,'" said Jo. "Christian's Celestial City is over there. Can you see the turreted castle waiting to receive the pilgrims? Wouldn't it be fun," she added, "if we could really live in the castles we make in the air?"

Laurie considered a moment as he made himself comfortable on the soft carpet of pine needles. "My air castle is to live abroad and to have just as much music as I choose. What's yours, Meg?"

"I should like to have a lovely house full of luxurious things—pleasant people and heaps of money," she said.

"Wouldn't you have a master for your mansion in the air?" asked Laurie slyly, for he knew a secret and wondered if Meg guessed it.

"I said 'pleasant people.' " Meg leaned to tie her shoe so that no one saw her face.

"Why don't you say you'd have a splendid husband," Jo said bluntly. "That's what you mean."

"You'd have nothing but horses, inkstands, and reams of paper in your air castle," Meg retorted, a little sharply.

"Wouldn't I though! A stable full of Arabian steeds and a magic inkstand. I shall write books and get rich and famous. That's my favorite dream. I've got the key to my castle in the air," Jo added, "but whether I can unlock the door remains to be seen." She spoke mysteriously and would answer none of their questions, for, like Laurie, she too had a secret. If only she could make her dream come true!

Dark Days

ONE dreary November day, Laurie appeared at the March house to take the girls for a drive.

He leaned over Mrs. March's chair affectionately. "Is there anything we can do for you on the way, ma'am?"

"No, thank you," Mrs. March answered.

A sharp ring at the door interrupted her, and a minute later Hannah came in with a telegram.

Mrs. March ripped it open and read:

Mrs. March:
Your husband is very ill. Come at once.
S. Hale
Blank Hospital, Washington

"I shall go at once," she said, "but it may be too late. Jo, run to the Aid Society and tell Mrs. King I can't come. Beth,

go ask Mr. Laurence for a couple of bottles of good wine. I'm not to proud to beg for Father."

Mr. Laurence came hurrying back with Beth, bringing every comfort he could think of. There was nothing Mr. Laurence didn't offer, from his own dressing gown to himself as escort.

At the thought of having an escort, Mrs. March's eyes brightened with relief. But she shook her head. "I cannot hear of your undertaking the long journey," she said firmly.

Mr. Laurence knit his brows, then marched abruptly out of the house. "Be back directly," he muttered.

No one had time to think of him again until Meg, coming through the hall with a pair of rubbers in one hand and a cup of tea in the other, came suddenly upon John Brooke, Laurie's tutor, who always made Meg feel shy and young.

"I came to offer myself as escort to your mother, Miss March. Mr. Laurence has business for me in Washington, and it will give me a great deal of satisfaction to be of service to her there."

Down dropped the rubbers, and the tea was very near to following, as Meg put out her hands. Mr. Brooke blushed with pleasure and embarrassment at her gratitude.

Dusk fell on the house before Jo finally came walking in. Without removing her bonnet or cloak, she laid a roll of bills before her mother, saying with a little choke in her voice, "That's my contribution toward making Father comfortable and bringing him home."

"My dear, where did you get it? Twenty-five dollars! Jo, I hope you haven't done anything rash?"

"No. I didn't beg, borrow, or steal it. I don't think you'll blame me, for I only sold what was my own."

As she spoke, Jo took off her bonnet. All of her long, thick chestnut hair was cut off.

"Your hair! Your beautiful hair!" Amy wailed.

"Oh, Jo, how could you? Your one beauty," whispered Meg.

"My dear girl," Mrs. March said with trembling lips, "there was no need of this."

Jo's indifferent air deceived no one. She rumpled up the short brown mop. "It doesn't affect the fate of the nation," she murmured stoutly. "I was getting too proud of my long hair. The barber said I could soon have a curly crop which will be boyish and easy to keep in order. I'm satisfied, so please take the money, and let's have supper."

"Didn't you feel dreadful when the cutting began?" Meg asked in a sympathetic voice.

"I'll confess I felt queer when I saw my hair laid out on the table," Jo answered. "The woman gave me a lock to keep. I'll give it to you, Marmee. Perhaps you'd like to keep it."

Mrs. March folded the wavy chestnut lock and laid it away in her desk. Something in her face made the girls change the subject to Mr. Brooke's kindness in going as escort and the happy times they'd have together when their father was brought home.

In the cold gray dawn, the lamps in the March household were lit. The big trunk was ready in the hall. Hannah flew about the kitchen with her nightcap on, making tea.

Laurie and his grandfather came in to see the travelers off, and Mr. Brooke looked so strong and sensible that the girls christened him "Mr. Greatheart" on the spot.

"Good-by, my darlings!" whispered Mrs. March. "God bless and keep us all!"

"I feel as if there had been an earthquake," said Jo, as the carriage rolled away and was lost to sight in the early morning fog. "It seems as if half the house were gone."

For the first week, each of the girls wrote long letters. They read in their little guidebooks, attended to their duties and, indeed, were models of virtue. Little by little, however, they began to fall back into the old ways. Only Beth seemed to take on her mother's outside duties as well as her share of the housekeeping.

One cold afternoon, when the older girls were comfortably toasting their toes by the fire, Beth quietly slipped out with a basket of food for the Hummel children.

It was late when she came back, and no one saw her go upstairs and shut herself in her mother's room. Half an hour later, Jo found her sitting near the medicine chest in her mother's closet. Her eyes were red from weeping, and she had a medicine bottle in her hand.

"Oh, Jo, the baby's dead!" Beth sobbed.

"What baby?"

"Mrs. Hummel's; it died in my lap before she got home. Then Mrs. Hummel came with the doctor."

"Don't cry, Beth."

"The doctor said the baby had had scarlet fever and he told me to go right home and take belladonna or I'd have the fever."

"No, you won't," cried Jo, hugging her close with a frightened look. "Beth, I'll never forgive myself if you get sick!"

Jo went to consult Hannah and Meg. "Now I'll tell you what we'll do," said Hannah calmly. "We'll have Dr. Bangs come to take a look at Beth. And we'll send Amy off to your Aunt March's for a spell to keep her out of harm's way. Jo can amuse Beth for a day or two. We'll keep her in bed."

Beth did have the fever and was much sicker than anyone but Hannah and Dr. Bangs suspected. Very little was known

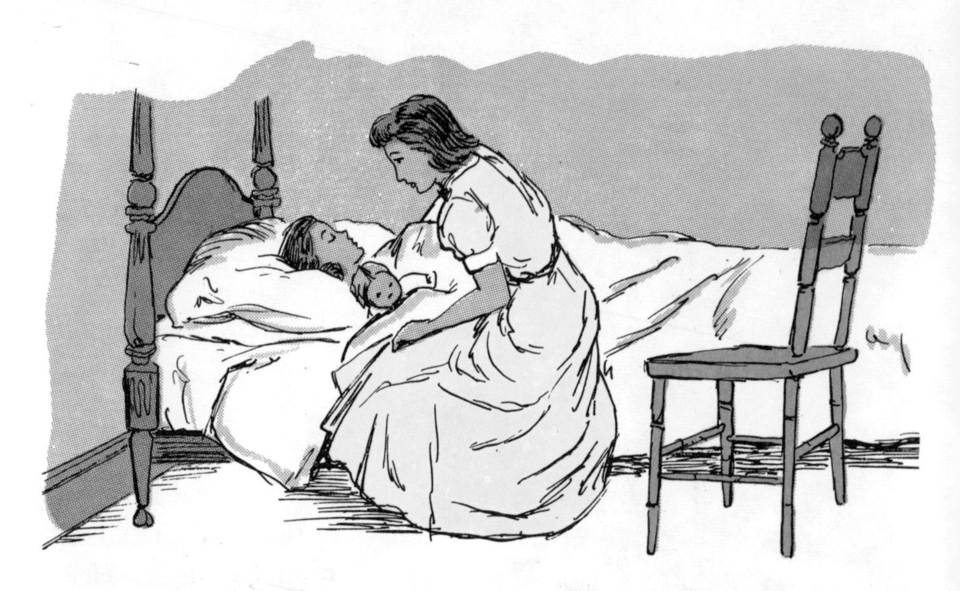

about scarlet fever. Dr. Bangs did his best, but left a good deal to Hannah's experienced nursing.

Hannah wouldn't hear of Mrs. March's being told. "Your father needs her, girls," she said, "and we can take care of Beth." So Meg and Jo wrote daily letters to Washington without any mention of the illness. They did not think it right to deceive their mother but had been bidden to obey.

A letter from Washington added to their anxiety, for their father was worse. How dark the days seemed, how heavy the hearts of the sisters as they worked and waited!

Dr. Bangs came twice a day, Hannah sat up at night, Meg kept a telegram ready to send her mother, but Hannah still said, "There's not any danger yet."

The first of December was a wintry, stormy day. When Dr. Bangs came that morning, he held Beth's hot hand in his a moment and laid it gently down, saying in a low tone to Hannah, "If Mrs. March *can* leave her husband, she'd better be sent for."

Jo ran to the parlor, snatched up the telegram, and rushed out into the storm to send the message.

She was just returning to the house when Laurie came in, bringing a letter which said that Mr. March was mending again. Jo looked up from reading it with a face so full of misery that Laurie asked quickly, "What is it? Is Beth worse?"

"I've sent for Mother."

"Good for you, Jo!"

"The doctor told us to."

"Oh, Jo, is it as bad as that?" Laurie looked startled.

As the tears streamed down poor Jo's cheeks, she stretched out her hand in a helpless sort of way. Laurie took it in his, saying, "I'm here. Hold on to me, Jo."

"I can't let Beth go, I can't, I can't," sobbed Jo.

"Beth is not going to die. I'm sure she's not," Laurie whispered. "And tonight, I'll give you something that will warm the cockles of your heart." Laurie spoke in such a strange tone that Jo looked up through her tears.

"What is it?" she cried.

"I telegraphed your mother yesterday, and Brooke answered that she'd come at once, and she'll be here tonight, and everything will be all right. Aren't you glad I did it?"

"Oh, Laurie, I am *so* glad," Jo cried, and threw her arms around his neck. "You were such a dear to do it."

"I got fidgety," Laurie said, "and so did Grandpa. When he said it was high time something was done, I pelted over to the telegraph office. The late train comes in at two in the morning. I shall go for your mother."

"Laurie, you're an angel! How shall I ever thank you?"

"Throw your arms around me again. I rather like it," answered Laurie with some of his old mischievousness.

But Jo vanished into the kitchen to tell Hannah.

"That's the interferingest boy I ever did see," Hannah said. "But I forgive him and do hope Mrs. March is coming on right away," she added.

Mrs. March Returns

WITH Laurie's news, a breath of fresh air seemed to blow through the house.

Everyone rejoiced but Beth. She lay in a heavy sleep, only rousing to mutter "Water!" with lips so parched they could hardly shape the word. Jo and Meg hovered over her as the snow fell; the bitter wind raged, and the hours dragged on.

At dusk, the doctor came in and said that some change, for better or worse, would probably take place about midnight, at which time he would return.

It was past two when the great change seemed to take place. The fever flush and the look of pain were gone, and the beloved little face looked pale and peaceful.

Soon, Dr. Bangs came to confirm the happy truth. He was homely, but Jo thought his face heavenly when he smiled and said, "Yes, my dears, I think the little girl will pull through. Keep the house quiet, let her sleep. When she wakes give her—"

What they were to give, neither heard. They held each other close with hearts too full for words.

Never had the sun risen so beautifully and never had the world seemed so lovely as it did to Meg and Jo as they looked out in the early morning. Meg brought Amy's rose that had blossomed in the night and put it in a little vase right by Beth's bed.

"When she wakes, the first thing she will see will be the little rose and Mother's face," she said softly.

"Listen!" cried Jo, starting to her feet. There was a sound of bells at the door below, a glad cry from Hannah, and then Laurie's voice: "Girls, she's come! She's come!"

Meg's wish was realized, for when Beth woke, the first objects on which her eyes fell were the little rose and her mother's face. Too weak to wonder at anything, she only smiled and slept again.

That evening while Meg was writing to her father, Jo slipped upstairs into Beth's room. She stood a minute by her mother's chair, twisting her fingers in her short curls with a worried gesture.

"What is the matter, Jo?" Mrs. March asked gently.

"I want to tell you something very important, Mother."

"About Meg?"

"How quickly you guessed!"

"When Meg left her gloves next door, only one was returned. Laurie told me Mr. Brooke had it. When Laurie teased him about it, Mr. Brooke said he cared for Meg but didn't dare say so because she was young and he was poor. Isn't that a dreadful situation?"

"Do you think Meg is interested in John?" Mrs. March asked calmly.

"*Who?*"

"Mr. Brooke. I call him John now. We fell into the way of doing so at the hospital, and he likes it."

"Oh, dear!" Jo cried. "I know you'll take his part."

"My dear, don't get angry about it. John went with me at Mr. Laurence's request. He was so devoted to your father that we couldn't help getting fond of him. He told us that he loved Meg but would earn a comfortable home before he asked her to marry him. I prefer not to say anything to Meg yet. When John comes back from the war and I see them together, I'll be able to judge better her feeling toward him."

"She'll see *his* feeling in those handsome brown eyes she talks about, and then it will be up with her," Jo said gloomily. "Brooke will carry her off and make a hole in the family. Everything will be horribly uncomfortable then, Mother." And Jo shook her fist at the absent John Brooke.

"Your father and I have agreed that Meg shall not be married before she is twenty. If she and John love one another, it is best that they wait and test their love for each other."

Jo gave her mother a hug. "I wish wearing flatirons on our heads would keep us from growing up. But buds will be roses and kittens, cats—more's the pity."

A Christmas Present

LIKE sunshine after storm were the peaceful weeks that followed. Mr. March began to write of returning early in the new year. Beth improved rapidly and was soon able to lie on the study sofa all day, amusing herself with the cats and her family of bedraggled dolls.

Several days of unusually fine weather ushered in a splendid Christmas Day. Beth, wrapped in her mother's gift—a soft, cherry-red dressing gown—was carried in triumph to the window to behold the offering of Jo and Laurie. They had made a stately snow maiden in the garden. Crowned with holly, she bore a basket of fruit in one hand and a great roll of new music in the other. A bright, woolly afghan was wrapped about her shoulders, and a pink paper streamer held this Christmas carol:

God bless you, dear Queen Bess!
May nothing you dismay,
But health and peace and happiness
Be yours, this Christmas Day.

"I'm so full of happiness," said Beth, "that if Father were only here, I couldn't hold a drop more."

Half an hour later Laurie opened the parlor door and popped his head in. He said very quietly, "Here's another Christmas present for the March family." He might just as well have given an Indian war whoop, for his face gave him away.

Before the words were out of his mouth, a tall man took his place, leaning heavily on the arm of another tall man. There was a general stampede as Mr. March became invisible in the embrace of loving arms. And for the next few minutes, everybody seemed to lose his wits. Jo nearly fainted and had to be comforted on Laurie's shoulder. Mr. Brooke kissed Meg entirely by mistake. Amy tumbled over a stool and, never stopping to get up, hugged her father's boots contentedly.

Suddenly Mrs. March remembered Beth, who had been carried to the next room to rest on the sofa. But joy had put strength into the feeble limbs. The little cherry-red wrapper appeared on the threshold, and Beth ran straight into her father's arms.

What a happy time it was! There never was such a Christmas dinner as they had that day.

Mr. Laurence and Laurie dined with them, and also Mr. Brooke —at whom Jo glowered darkly. As twilight gathered, the guests departed, and the happy family sat together around the fire.

"This year has been rather a rough road for you to have traveled, my little pilgrims," Mr. March said. "But you have got on bravely."

"How did you know? Did Mother tell you?" asked Jo.

"A little, and I've made several discoveries today." Mr. March took Meg's hand. "Here's one," he said. "I remember when your first care was to keep your hands white and smooth. They were pretty then, but to me much prettier now, for I read usefulness in these hands."

"What about Jo? Please say something nice," whispered Beth in her father's ear.

"In spite of the curly crop, I don't see the tomboy I left a year ago," said Mr. March. "I rather miss my wild girl, but I am proud to have a strong, helpful, tender-hearted woman in her place."

Jo's thin face grew rosy in the firelight as she received her father's praise.

"Now Beth," said Amy, longing for her own turn.

Mr. March just held the little girl close. "I've got you safe, my Beth, and I'll keep you so, please God."

After a minute's silence he looked down at Amy. "I observed that Amy took drumsticks at dinner, though she prefers the breast. I also observe that she does not think so often of her looks, so I conclude that she has learned to think more of other people and less of herself."

Beth slipped from her father's arms and went slowly to her little piano and, for the first time in many weeks, touched the keys. As they had always done in times past, the reunited family closed the day with a song.

The Future Begins

ON THE DAY after Christmas, the whole household had trouble settling down. The girls hovered about their father like bees near clover.

Questions that needed to be answered were in the air. Jo was seen to shake her fist at Mr. Brooke's umbrella, which had been left in the hall. Meg jumped when the bell rang and colored when John's name was mentioned.

"If John did speak," Jo said accusingly, "you'd cry or blush and let him have his own way instead of giving a good, decided 'No.' "

"Not at all. I should say quite calmly, 'Thank you, Mr. Brooke, you are very kind, but I agree with my father that I am too young to enter into any engagement at present. So please say no more, but let us be friends as we were.' Then I'd walk out of the room with dignity."

Meg was about to rehearse the dignified exit when a tap on

the door made her fly into her seat and begin to sew as if her life depended on it.

"Good afternoon," said John Brooke shyly, "I came to get my umbrella. That is, I came to see how your father is. That is—"

"It's very well, he's in the rack. I'll get him, and tell it you're here," Jo mumbled, and having mixed her father and John's umbrella together, she slipped out of the room to give Meg a chance to make her speech.

But the instant they were alone, Meg moved toward the door. "Pray sit down. I'll tell Mother you're here."

"Don't go," Mr. Brooke said. "Are you afraid of me, Margaret?"

Meg blushed up to the little curls on her forehead. "How can I be afraid of you when you have been so kind to Father? I only wish I could thank you for it."

"Shall I tell you how?" asked John, taking her small hand in his and looking down at her with so much love that her heart began to flutter.

"Oh, no, please don't—I'd rather not," she whispered.

"I only want to know if you can care for me just a little, Meg. You see, I love you very much."

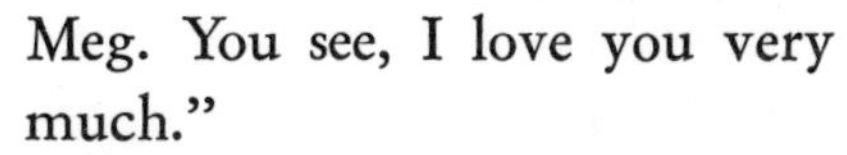

This was the moment for the calm, cold speech that Meg had prepared, but she forgot every word of it. She hung her head and answered, "I don't know," so softly that John had to stoop down to catch the foolish little reply.

"I'll wait and in the meantime, could you be learning to

like me? Would it be a very hard lesson?" And he took possession of her other hand.

"Not if I chose to learn, but—" In her confusion she cried, "But I don't choose. Please go away!"

Poor John looked as if his castle in the air had tumbled about his ears. "Do you really mean that?" he asked anxiously.

"Yes, I do," Meg murmured and walked away.

John was pale and grave now. There is no telling what might have happened next if Aunt March had not come hobbling into the parlor, unannounced.

Meg turned scarlet, and John vanished through the study door in three strides.

"Bless me, what's all this!" cried the old lady, with a rap of her cane.

"Mr. Brooke came for his umbrella," Meg began lamely—

"Umbrella, eh? Brooke? That boy's tutor? I understand now. I know all about it. Jo blurted it out by mistake one day. You haven't gone and accepted him, child?"

"Hush! He'll hear you," Meg whispered, much troubled.

"Don't care if he does. I've something to say to you, and I must free my mind at once. Do you mean to marry this—Cook? If you do, not one penny of my money ever goes to you. Remember that and be a sensible girl."

If Aunt March had begged her grandniece to accept John Brooke, Meg probably would have declared she couldn't think of it. Upon being ordered not to like him, she replied with unusual spirit, "I shall marry whom I please, Aunt March, and you can leave your money to anyone you wish."

"Highty tighty! You ought to catch a rich husband and help your family."

"Father and Mother don't think so," Meg answered, feeling brave and independent. "They like John, though he is poor."

"This Rook is poor? I thought as much!"

"I couldn't do better if I waited half my life! John is good and wise. Everyone likes and respects him, and I'm proud to think he cares for me," said Meg, looking prettier than ever.

"He knows *you* have rich relations. That's why he has come a-courting."

"Aunt March, how dare you say such a thing!" Meg cried.

The old lady was very angry. "I wash my hands of you. Don't expect anything from me when you are married to your Mr. Book!" With that, she stamped out of the house and slammed the door.

Left alone, Meg stood a moment, undecided whether to laugh or cry. Before she could make up her mind, John was at her side. "I couldn't help hearing. Thank you for defending me. Then you *do* care for me a little."

Here was another chance for Meg's well-planned speech and dignified exit. Instead she hid her face in his waistcoat and whispered, "Yes, John."

Fifteen minutes later, Jo came downstairs, paused at the parlor door, and hearing no sound, nodded with satisfaction. "She has sent him away and that affair is settled!" She opened the door prepared to praise her strong-minded sister and crow over a fallen enemy. It was certainly a shock to behold the enemy sitting on the sofa with the strong-minded sister on his knee!

Jo rushed out of the room and up the stairs to her parents. "Do go down quickly!" she exclaimed tragically. "John Brooke is acting dreadfully, and Meg likes it!"

Mr. and Mrs. March did go down to the parlor, and a great deal of quiet talking and planning was done. Jo got little comfort from Beth and Amy when she told them the awful news, so she went up to her refuge in the garret and poured out her troubles to Scrabble and his friends.

The tea bell brought her down at last, and John and Meg looked so happy that she hadn't the heart to show how dismal she felt.

Just then Laurie came prancing in with a bridal-looking bouquet for "Mrs. John Brooke." "I knew John would have his way," he said, acting as if he thought he had made the match.

After a moment he drew Jo to the corner by the window. "You don't look festive," he said gently.

"It can never be the same. I just can't give Meg up," mourned Jo.

The boy put his hand on her shoulder. "You don't give her up. You only go halves," consoled Laurie. "And you've got me anyhow. I'm not good for much, I know. But I'll stand by you, Jo, for all the days of my life." And Laurie meant what he said.

How It All Turned Out

"DON'T you wish you could look into the future and see what's going to happen to us all?" Laurie asked.

Jo shook her head. "Everyone is so happy now, I don't believe they could be much improved. And I might see something sad."

The three years before Meg's marriage passed quickly. John Brooke spent a year on the battlefields with the Union Army, was wounded and sent home. As soon as he recovered his health, he set about finding work and earning money to make a home for his bride. It was Laurie, now a dashing college man, who named their little brown house the "Dovecote," for he said that Meg and John went about building like a pair of turtledoves.

Even Jo had to admit that if one must have a wedding, Meg's was perfect. The parlor of the March home was decorated with garlands. Meg made her white muslin dress herself, and the only ornaments she wore were lilies of the valley, John's favorite flower.

There was no bridal procession. When Aunt and Uncle Carrol and the cousins, Laurie and Mr. Laurence, and a few other friends were seated in the parlor, Mr. March and the young couple took their places under the green-garlanded arch. The sisters and their mother drew close.

All three girls wore suits of thin silvery gray, and pink roses in their hair. Jo's curly crop had lengthened into a thick coil. At nineteen her boyish angles had softened, and she carried herself with ease. Beth had grown slender and pale. Though she seldom complained and always spoke hopefully of getting better soon, the shadow of her illness never quite left her beautiful eyes. Amy, though she was only sixteen, had the bearing and grace of a full-grown woman. Her nose still afflicted her because it never *would* grow Grecian, as she had hoped for so long, but she consoled herself with her fair complexion, keen blue eyes, and golden curls.

The only bridal journey Meg had was the quiet walk with John from her old home to the new. But it was nevertheless a new world into which she entered. When the first year rolled around, twin babies were born—a girl and a boy—who soon became great favorites with all the Marches.

Jo's passion for independence had grown, and she was sure that in her writing she held the key to making her air castle come true. The garret saw more and more of her, as she worked on her novel or turned out romances for the weekly newspapers. At last she had a real success when a letter arrived from an editor who had offered a prize of a hundred dollars for a romantic tale. A prouder young woman was seldom seen, for, on opening the letter, a check for the prize money fell into her lap.

But money to help in the household was only a part of Jo's air castle. She wanted the satisfaction and fame of serious authorship, too. So she worked hard and finished her novel and

actually found a publisher for it. When the book came out, it met with as much blame as praise, and Jo needed all the comfort her family and Laurie could bestow to bear the trials of being "an authoress."

Poor Jo had another disappointment at this time which was even harder to bear. The Carrols were going to Europe for a year, and Aunt March arranged to send one of her grandnieces along. Jo had always longed to travel abroad, to see with her own eyes the wonders of Paris and London and Rome that she had read about so hungrily. But it was Amy who received the invitation. Jo bore up until the day the Laurence carriage rolled away to take Amy to the ship. Then she retired to the garret and cried until she couldn't cry any more.

Amy had been in raptures at her good fortune, but now that the time for leaving was at hand, she realized how far away she was going and for how long a time. She clung to Laurie at the dock, saying with a sob, "Oh, take care of them for me, and if anything should happen—"

"If anything happens, I'll come and comfort you," whispered Laurie, little dreaming that he would be called on to keep his word.

Laurie's devotion to each one of the March girls had never

wavered, but, for Jo, his feelings were more than brotherly. Jo would stand for "no nonsense," however, and cut him short whenever he tried to express his feelings. She decided to go away for a while, hoping that he would fasten his affection on someone more suitable. "Beth would be just right for him," she said to herself. "If I went away, he might find it out!" And forthwith she won her parents' permission to take a job in New York as governess to the children of her mother's old friend, Mrs. Kirke.

She was soon installed on the top floor of Mrs. Kirke's boarding house. Her letters home were bright and cheerful, but Jo spent many lonely hours that winter.

She would have been lonelier still but for the friendship of one of Mrs. Kirke's boarders—a wise, bumbling, kindly professor of German. Professor Bhaer lived with his two young, motherless nephews in the big room next to her own. In Germany he had been a well-known and honored scholar. Here in New York he was just one of many struggling foreigners, barely making enough to live on. But poor as he was, Friedrich Bhaer had within himself such richness of mind and spirit, such humor and gaiety, that everyone loved him.

Jo spent many pleasant hours with the professor, exploring the great city with her charges and his nephews, and discovering the whole world of German literature and music.

Grateful for the professor's friendship, Jo did not guess until long afterward what she gave in return. At forty, the professor was still unmarried, for it had never before been his fortune to find a girl like Jo. He hesitated to speak of his affection, hesitated even to hope, after something Jo said on the last day of her stay in New York.

"You must come and see us, if you travel our way," she urged warmly. "I want my family to know my new friend."

"Do you? Shall I come?" he asked eagerly.

"Yes, come next month. Laurie graduates from college then. You will enjoy an American commencement."

The eagerness disappeared from the professor's voice. "Laurie? That is your best friend of whom you speak?"

"Yes, my boy. I'm very proud of him. You'll come?"

The good man shook his head. "She is not for me, I must not hope it now," he said to himself sorrowfully. But aloud, to Jo, he only said, "I wish the friend much success and you, all happiness. God bless you," he added, and turned away.

In the winter that Jo was gone, Laurie had applied himself soberly to his studies, determined that when he graduated she should be proud of him. And she *was* proud and happy in his companionship again. But Laurie was not ready to play the brotherly role as before.

"It's no good, Jo," he said. "We've got to have it out. I've loved you ever since I've known you. I've tried to show it, but you wouldn't let me. Now I'm going to make you hear and give me an answer. Don't disappoint us—my grandfather and Beth and everyone expects us—I know that I'm not half good enough—"

"Yes, you are! Oh, of course you are, Laurie!" cried Jo, finding it a good deal harder to refuse Laurie than she had expected.

But she did refuse, for the love she felt for the dark-eyed, handsome boy was that of a good friend but not of a wife. Sorrowfully she saw him leave with his grandfather for the year in Europe they had talked about so often.

Jo had little time to regret her decision though, for Beth claimed all her attention now. When Jo came home from New York, she had been struck by the change in the gentle girl, and an unspoken fear had clutched her heart. Beth seemed to have a secret that Jo guessed but refused to put a name to. She waited for her sister to speak, waited and watched as Beth grew paler and quieter. Finally in midsummer Jo took her to the seashore. Perhaps by the ocean, Beth would regain her strength and health.

One day as they rested on the rocky beach, Beth reached out her feeble hand and touched Jo's strong, brown cheek. The concern in the older girl's eyes was too plain to ignore. "Jo, dear, I'm glad you know," Beth murmured. "I've tried hard to tell you that I know I will never get well. I've known since last autumn. Don't be troubled, dear. It's best, indeed it is."

"I won't give you up!" cried Jo rebelliously. "You *must* get well. What will we do without you?"

"Meg has John and the babies, but you must stand by Father and Mother, won't you, Jo? And Amy—dear little girl—I hope I shall see her again."

"She's coming next spring, and I mean to have you well by that time," Jo began. But Beth stopped her. "Jo, dear, don't hope any more. It won't do any good. Let us have happy times while we wait."

Somehow the family found courage to give Beth this last wish. The months that followed *were* made happy, though the shadow of death was upon them. The end came in the early spring as naturally and as simply as sleep.

To be brave and cheerful for Beth's sake had not been hard while she was with them, but the weeks and months following her sister's death were, for Jo, dark days indeed.

Laurie had visited Amy in Italy at Christmas time and had been a pleasant enough dancing partner, but Amy was dismayed by the change in him. Wrapped up in her own affairs, she was slow to discover the reason for the boy's low spirits. Of her own problems, she had written home very frankly. Fred Vaughn, an English friend of the Laurences, had called on her in London and then had appeared again in Italy. He was attractive and rich and could give her all the things she thought she wanted. She was not in love with Fred, but if he asked her to marry him when he returned in the spring, she intended to say yes.

Laurie questioned her about Fred with brotherly concern.

"He's rich and has delightful manners," Amy answered. "And I could be fond of him if I tried."

"I understand," Laurie observed lazily. "Queens of society can't get on without money. But I would not have expected this from one of your mother's girls."

These words ruffled Amy, and she turned on Laurie with a rare show of temper. It was not until she had scolded him roundly for his own aimless life that she stumbled on the reason for his discouragement. "I'm sorry," Amy said, "but I can't help wishing that you'd bear your disappointment better. Why don't you do something splendid and *make* Jo love you? If not that, then learn to forget."

The frank words on both sides rankled; but truth had been spoken in that little quarrel and when they were apart again, both Amy and Laurie were honest enough to admit it. Fred did return and ask Amy to marry him. Without regret, she sent him away. Meanwhile, Laurie had taken Amy's advice and tried to do something "splendid" with his music. He spent the winter in Vienna composing a tragic piece that was intended to stir Jo's soul. But somehow, Amy's pretty face and her new charm came between him and his tragic "Requiem." He found himself composing a sprightly opera instead, with a golden-haired heroine in a white dress and silver bangles. He had thought the task of forgetting his "hopeless love" would take years. To his surprise he found it growing easier every day. Then came the short, grief-stricken note from Jo telling of Beth's death. His first thought was for Amy, so far from her family in this sorrow. He deserted his music and went to her at once in Switzerland.

Amy clung to Laurie and her need of him brought out a strength and manliness that Jo's independence had never done. Amy no longer scolded Laurie, and in the days that followed did everything to please him, for she found that her fondness for the boy next door had ripened into a warm, sweet love. When the Carrols decided to extend their stay in Europe, Laurie and Amy were quietly married in Paris and, with old Mr. Laurence, set out on the homeward journey.

At home, Jo remained in the Slough of Despond. Even her writing brought no comfort, and except for one poem about Beth, no words came from her pen. The verses were not very good, but they came from a full heart. More from habit than anything else, she had sent them to a New York newspaper that printed a good deal of poetry. Though the poem was signed only with her initials, one loving pair of eyes recognized that the sorrowful lines were hers and that she was troubled.

On the very evening that Amy and Laurie returned with their tremendous news—for the marriage had been kept as a surprise—while all the family were gathered to admire and wonder, there came a knock on the Marches' door. Jo opened it, and Professor Bhaer stood beaming at her from the darkness.

If the good man had any doubt about his welcome, a look at Jo's face dispelled it as she drew him into the family circle.

The professor's visit lasted a fortnight. When he realized that Laurie was no longer "Jo's boy," it gave him courage to ask one day as they walked together in the rain, "Can you find a little place in your heart for poor, old Fritz?"

"Oh, yes!" cried Jo immediately, never caring whether it was proper or not to kiss her professor under the umbrella.

"I'm to carry my share and help earn the home," she explained later to her family, "while Fritz teaches at the college out West. We love one another, and that will make waiting easier."

But the wait was not as long as they had expected. Aunt March died suddenly the following year, and in her will left Plumfield, the large, rambling country home of the March family, to Jo.

"You'll sell the place, of course, and then you'll have enough to marry your professor," said Laurie, as they all sat talking of Jo's good fortune.

"Not at all!" Jo replied. "Fritz and I shall open a school for boys—for rich and poor, for strong and lame, for white and black—a good, happy, homelike school. Bless Fritz's dear heart; he's been helping poor boys all his life. With my professor and Father to teach them and myself to romp with them and scold them and pet them, and all of you to stand by and give us sage advice—I'm sure we can do it."

"Of course you can," Meg agreed.

"It's a splendid idea, and it's just like Jo to think of it," added Amy warmly.

Mrs. March pressed her husband's hand and said softly, "How happy I am that the last of our little women has found her purpose in life."